WE'RE ALL WONDERS

WRITTEN AND ILLUSTRATED BY **R. J. PALACIO**

PUFFIN BOOKS
UK | USA | Canada | Ireland | Australia
India | New Zealand | South Africa
Puffin Books is part of the Penguin Random House group of companies
whose addresses can be found at global.penguinrandomhouse.com.

www.penguin.co.uk   www.puffin.co.uk   www.ladybird.co.uk

Penguin
Random House
UK

Published in Great Britain by Puffin Books 2017
001

Printed in Italy

A CIP catalogue record for this book is available from the British Library

ISBN: 978–0–141–38641–6

All correspondence to:
Puffin Books, Penguin Random House Children's
80 Strand, London WC2R 0RL

A note on the art in this book: I based Auggie's look in this picture book on the iconic jacket
for *Wonder*, which was art-directed by Isabel Warren-Lynch and beautifully envisioned and
drawn by the artistic wonder Tad Carpenter. I am ever thankful for their collaboration,
which resulted in an image that has captured the imagination of readers everywhere. I drew
all the line art for these illustrations with an iPencil in Procreate for the iPad, and used
a combination of painting (with the stylus) and Photoshop to create the final art.

For Nathaniel Newman, a true wonder,
and his wonder of a family, Magda, Russel, and Jake.

For Dina Zuckerberg and the MyFace family.
You are my heroes.

I know I'm not an ordinary kid.

Sure, I do ordinary things.

I ride a bike.

I eat ice cream.

I play ball.

I just don't look ordinary.

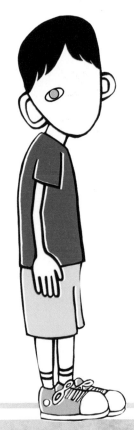

I don't look like other kids.

My mum says I'm unique.
She says I'm a wonder.

My dog, Daisy, agrees!

But some people don't see
that I'm a wonder.

All they see
is how different I look.

Sometimes they
stare at me.

They point or laugh.

They even say
mean things
behind my back.

But I can hear them.

It hurts my feelings.

It hurts Daisy's feelings, too.

When that happens, I put on my helmet.

I put Daisy's helmet on, too. And then we…

BLAST OFF!

Up! Up! Up!
Up through the clouds…

across the galaxy...

...all the way to Pluto!

We say hello to old friends.

From far away, the Earth looks so small. I can't see any people. But I know they're there.

Billions of people. People of all different colours. People who walk and talk differently. People who look different. Like me!

The Earth is big enough for all kinds of people.

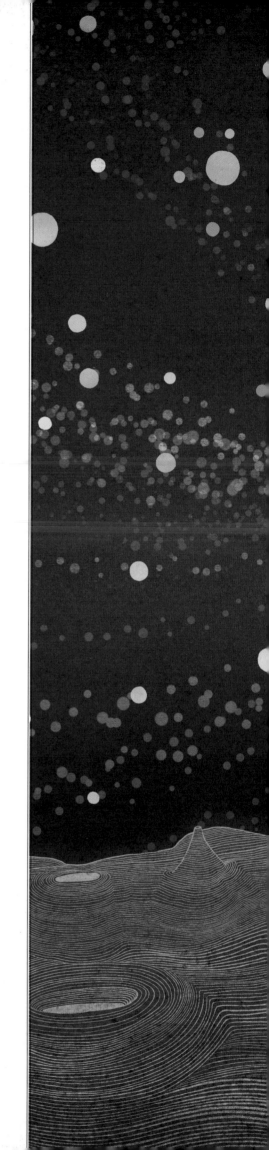

I know I can't change the way I look.

But maybe, just maybe...

...people can change the way they see.

If they do, they'll see that I'm a wonder.

And they'll see that they're wonders, too.

We're all wonders!

Look with kindness and you will always find wonder.